DINO RIDDLES

by Katy Hall and Lisa Eisenberg

pictures by Nicole Rubel

PUFFIN BOOKS

PUFFIN BOOKS
Published by Penguin Group
Penguin Young Readers Group,
345 Hudson Street, New York, New York 10014, U.S.A.
Penguin Books Ltd, 80 Strand, London WC2R ORL, England
Penguin Books Australia Ltd, 250 Camberwell Road, Camberwell, Victoria 3124, Australia
Penguin Books Canada Ltd, 10 Alcorn Avenue, Toronto, Ontario, Canada M4V 3B2
Penguin Books (N.Z.) Ltd, 182-190 Wairau Road, Auckland 10, New Zealand

First published in the United States of America by
Dial Books for Young Readers, a division of Penguin Putnam Inc., 2002
Published by Puffin Books, a division of Penguin Young Readers Group, 2003

1 3 5 7 9 10 8 6 4 2

THE LIBRARY OF CONGRESS HAS CATALOGED THE DIAL BOOKS FOR YOUNG READERS EDITION AS FOLLOWS:
Hall, Katy.
Dino riddles / by Katy Hall and Lisa Eisenberg; pictures by Nicole Rubel.
p. cm.
Summary: A collection of riddles relating to dinosaurs, such as "What do you get
if you cross a dinosaur with a rabbit? Tricera*hops*!" and
"What do dinosaur campers cook over the fire? Dino-*s'mores*!"
ISBN: 0-8037-2239-7 (hc)
1. Riddles, Juvenile. 2. Dinosaurs—Juvenile humor.
[1. Dinosaurs—Wit and humor. 2. Riddles. 3. Jokes.]
I. Eisenberg, Lisa. II. Rubel, Nicole, ill. III. Title.
PN6371.5.H3477 2002
818'.5402—dc21 97-49947 CIP AC

Puffin Books ISBN 0-14-250179-4
Manufactured in China

The paintings, which consist of black ink and colored markers,
are color-separated and reproduced in full color.

Reading Level 2.6

To Joshua Mactey-don and
Zachary Tricera-schwabs

L.E.

To Ripton Gruss Rosen and
Morgan Gruss Rosen

K.H.

To all the little dinos

N.R.

What do you call a dinosaur in a cowboy hat and spurs?

Tyrannosaurus Tex.

How can you tell if a dinosaur
is a meat-eater or a plant-eater?

Lie down on a plate and see what happens!

What do you call a sleeping
dinosaur?

A Stego-*snore*-us.

Who always has change for a dollar?

A *Dime*-o-saur.

What do you get if you cross a
T. Rex with another T. Rex?

Don't do it! T. Rexes hate to be
double-crossed!

When did the Raptor cross
the street?

When the sign said "Stalk."

How did a stone-age wrecking crew blast through mountains?

With *dino*-mite!

Which dinosaur plays a mean boogie-woogie?

*Piano*saurus Rex.

What do dinosaurs put on their valentines before they mail them?

Stomps.

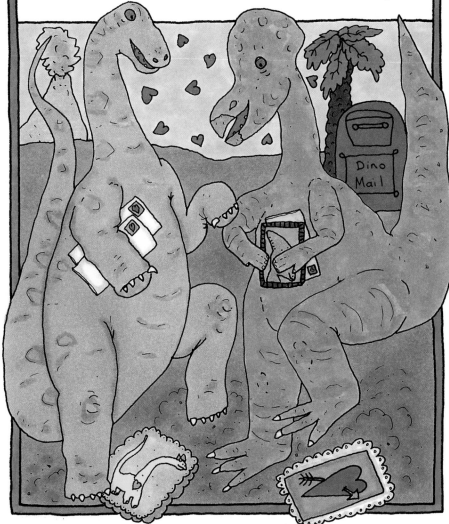

Where does Triceratops find
the best fries in town?

At the *diner*saur!

Why was Stegosaurus the star
of her volleyball team?

She could really *spike* the ball!

Which dinosaur never quits?

Tryceratops.

What did the dinosaur do at the rodeo?

He rode a bucking *Bronco*saurus!

What did the little dinosaur get
for her birthday?

A *Toy*rannosaurus Rex.

Which giant reptile has magic powers?

The Dino*sorcerer*.

What's the best way to raise a baby dinosaur?

With a crane.

Do any of the dinosaurs have trunks?

Only the ones who go on vacation!

What did the other dinosaurs think of Stegosaurus's new clothes?

They thought he looked really *sharp*.

What should you do if you see a blue dinosaur?

Cheer him up!

What do you get if you cross a fierce dinosaur and a giraffe?

A Tyrannosaurus Necks.

What did the Raptors say when the volcano erupted?

"What a *lava*ly day!"

What did the little dinosaur say when she had three tests to study for?

"I'm swamped!"

What do you get if you cross a
dog with a flying reptile?

A *Terrier*dactyl.

Which dinosaurs have helmets?

The ones in the motorcycle gang!

What did the little dinosaurs say to the big dinosaur when she went into the swamp?

"Wade for us!"

What did the dinosaur put on his barbecued ribs?

Dino*sauce*.

What do you get if you cross a dinosaur with a rabbit?

Tricera*hops*!

What do dinosaurs have that no other animal has?

Baby dinosaurs.

What did the Tyrannosaurus Rex do when she saw the perfect bathing suit?

She snapped it up!

Which dinosaur was a big hit at the Jurassic Halloween party?

The *Terror*dactyl.

What do dinosaur campers
cook over the fire?

Dino-*s'mores*!

Should you ever write a book
on dinosaurs?

No! You should write a book on paper!

What do you call a T. Rex who tries to find out secrets?

*Spy*rannosaurus Rex.

What kind of bedtime story do dinosaurs like best?

Tall *tails*!